Down East

Seven Days of Daisy

by Jamie Hogan

For Nana
7 years is not so long
after all

This island is where I live. It's a big rock in a blue bay. Every day is a new day.

My nana is coming for a visit in one week.
"What's a week?" I wonder.
"Seven days," my mom says.
"Is that a long time?" I ask.
She hangs a calendar near my bed.
Then she says, "It will go by fast, Daisy."

On Sunday I sail with Maeve and our dads. The sky and sea are wide and free. Clouds make a parade over our heads. When we pass Pumpkin Knob, I gobble my snack. The waves rock me like a baby in a cradle.

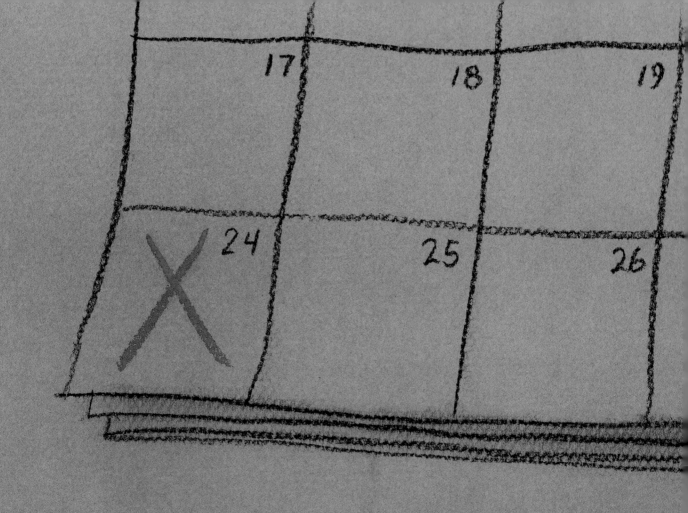

Before bedtime, I cross off the first day of the week.

One box is a long time.

On Monday Charles and I pretend monsters
are kayaking to Catnip Island. We hide behind
rocks and spy on the tall ships in the bay. I lose
my yellow binoculars.

I make a wish on the moon. I wish for the five days left until Nana's visit to go by fast. And that I will find my binoculars.

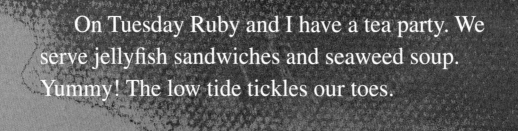

On Tuesday Ruby and I have a tea party. We
serve jellyfish sandwiches and seaweed soup.
Yummy! The low tide tickles our toes.

When the sun gets low, more friends come along. We throw off our clothes and dance in the tide pools. I find a piece of blue and yellow rope for my flotsam and jetsam collection. I'll show this to Nana! *Now* how many days?

SUNDAY	MONDAY	TUESDAY	WEDNESDAY	THURSDAY	FRIDAY	SATURDAY
					1	2
3	4	5	6	7	8	9
10	11	12	13	14	15	16
17	18	19	20	21 Flag Day	22	23
24 ✗ Father's Day	25 ✗	26 ✗	27	28		30

MAY
S M T W T F S
1 2 3 4 5
6 7 8 9 10 11 12
13 14 15 16 17 18 19
20 21 22 23 24 25 26
27 28 29 30 31

JULY
S M T W T F S
1 2 3 4 5 6 7
8 9 10 11 12 13 14
15 16 17 18 19 20 21
22 23 24 25 26 27 28
29 30 31

On Wednesday I walk
all the way to Whaleback
with my dad. The waves
spray my face.

I notice the seagulls having a meeting. "What do they talk about?" I wonder.

"Who knows," my dad says. I bet they talk about bagels.

At bedtime I make up a story about a whale named Wink giving me a ride around Spar Cove to meet a lobster family down below. Nana will love this story.

Thursday is good for thinking up silly names, like Foxy Chop and Noodly. I play tag with my mom under the oak tree and then just rock in the hammock, thinking and thinking. What if Nana misses the boat?

I see Fiona on the ferry on Friday. Captain Shawn lets us sit up in the wheelhouse.

He says, "Passengers on deck may want to cover their ears. Here comes a loud blast from the horn!"

We get groceries for Nana's visit.
On the boat ride home, I get giggly in
the fog.

After dark, my family walks
backshore to see the full moon.

I spot fireflies! I
want to catch them
all, but the mosquitoes
start biting.

On Saturday I spit watermelon
seeds with Susan. We tippy-toe
around the edge of the yard and her
kittens chase us.

Before dinner, I swing and sing songs like
"Polly Wolly Doodle" and "Choo Choo Boogaloo".

I dream about all seven days. A whole week
is not too long, I think. Tomorrow I will tell Nana
all about it.

ISBN 978-0-89272-919-7

Printed in Singapore

4   3   2   1

BOOKS·MAGAZINE·ONLINE
w w w . d o w n e a s t . c o m

Distributed to the trade by National Book Network

Library of Congress Cataloging-in-Publication Data